This book belongs to:

_____

_____

My dad wears polka-Dotted SOCKS!

Story by Kristin Joy Humes   Illustrations by Loel Barr

MERRY LANE PRESS

For Zane and Ruby

—Kristin Joy Humes

For Alex and Jessica

—Loel Barr

Merry Lane Press, a children's book publisher,
educates, entertains, and expands children's understanding
of the world in which they live.

Merry Lane Press also encourages our family of talented
individuals to explore new horizons and embrace new ideas.

Library of Congress Control Number: 2004116181
ISBN 0-9744307-2-2

Printed in China

For more information about our books, and the authors and artists
who create them, e-mail us at: alan@merrylanepress.com, or
visit our website: www.merrylanepress.com.

Merry Lane Press, 18 E. 16th Street, New York, NY 10003

One day, my teacher, Ms. Jenny, asked
everyone in the class to draw a picture of their
family to share at group time the following
day. Seems like an easy assignment, right?
No big deal, right? It wouldn't be—if I had a
normal family . . .

But I don't. My family is weird. When no one else is looking, we do strange things.

In the morning, my dad sings while he's in the shower. Then he eats breakfast wearing only his underwear and orange polka-dotted socks. When he comes home from work, he changes into a silly outfit playing something called yoga all by himself in the front yard. I just know that one day the neighbors will see him.

My mom likes to pretend she is a ghost. At nighttime, she puts white slime all over her face and white gloves on her hands. Then she dresses up in a white gown before she gets in bed. She doesn't seem to care when none of us act scared. What's the point of being a ghost if you're not even scary?

My sister Stella is three and half years
old. She eats dirt. Using a toy spoon, she scoops
the dirt from mom's garden and serves it to her
dolls. She always asks me if I'd like a spoonful.

My big brother Chase is almost eight years old.
He still takes his blanky to bed. When I'm seven,

I'm probably the closest thing to normal in my house. But there was that one time when I dressed up in mom's ghost outfit when she was out. But don't tell anyone. These are some of my family's secrets. It gets worse.

I have two dads, not one. The dad I live with is my stepdad. My real dad lives somewhere else and visits me on the weekends. He does wild things like skydiving, bungee jumping, and scuba diving. My parents told me that Chase, my brother, is only my half-brother. He looks whole to me. I don't get it.

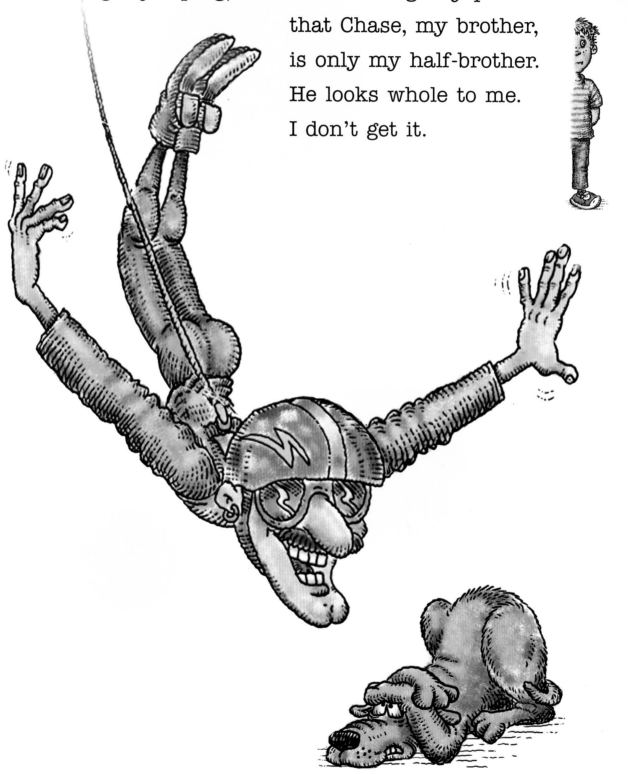

Even my aunts and uncles are strange. My Aunt
Ruby wears black shiny clothes and smells like our car.
She rides her motorcycle hundreds of miles to visit me.
When she gets here, she kisses me a thousand times.
Once would be plenty.

My Uncle Brad thinks that he's a pirate. He wears a patch on his eye and lives on a sailboat that doesn't ever move away from the dock. What kind of person lives on a broken boat?

I don't know what to do. I don't want to lie. But I
can't tell my family's secrets! The kids with normal
families will think I'm weird, too.

Even though my mom is a bit kooky, I've decided to
ask her what she would do. She usually is good at helping
me to solve problems. "Honey, all families are different,"
she says. "That's what makes them special."

The next day at school, all the kids sit fidgeting on the rug at group time with their drawings on their laps. Ms. Jenny asks who wants to go first.

Maggie raises her hand high. She always volunteers to go first. Maggie skips up to the front of the class. She points to her drawing. "Here's me, and here is my mom, and my dad, and my little brother, and my big sister." Then Maggie sits down.

I knew it! Mom was wrong! Everyone in Maggie's picture is normal. No secrets. The kids clapped for Maggie.

I slump down into the rug. I figure that if I make myself as small as possible Ms. Jenny will forget to call on me.

Larry goes up next. He has a big bouncy grin.
He did his drawing on a brown paper bag instead of
white paper. "This is my mother. She does karate."
Karate? Moms don't do karate!

"I have two dads. My real dad is an opera singer. He has to wear make-up and funny costumes when he sings."

Make up? Dads can't wear make-up!

"My stepdad is a writer. He writes scary books for grown ups."

"And this is me in the middle. Sometimes I think that my family is weird. My dad says that's what makes us special."

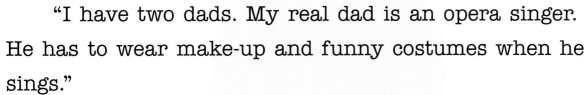

Larry's family is not so normal. And he has two dads,
too, like me. The kids are all clapping! So I clap the loudest.
The teacher looks around at all the kids on the rug.
I slump down as small as I can. Ms. Jenny's eyes stop at me.
"Hmmmm. Jake, would you like to go next?"

I slither up to the front. My heart is beating fast. What if the kids laugh? What if the teacher decides to send me home because she thinks a kid with such a weird family should not be allowed in school?

I hold up my picture. I had to use two sheets of paper. My mom helped me tape them together.

"This is my mom. She's-she-she takes care of me and my brother and sister. This is my stepdad. He works hard all day at work. This is my real dad. He goes on lots of adventures. This is my brother, Chase. He's almost eight. And this is my little sister, Stella. She likes to play in the garden."

Everyone is looking at me. The teacher is smiling. It is very quiet.

I take a deep breath and point at Uncle Brad. "And this is my Uncle Brad. He lives on a boat. It's broken," I say quietly, hoping no one can hear.

No one is laughing. I can't believe it.

"Cool!" says Joey, the class bully.

Feeling brave, I speak a little louder. "This is my Aunt Ruby. She rides motorcycles and smells like gasoline."

Maggie raises her hand. "Yes, Maggie?" asks Ms. Jenny.

"That's cool that your Aunt Ruby rides a motorcycle," says Maggie.

Ms. Jenny smiles. "Yes, Jake. What a wonderful family you have." Everyone claps.

Everyone, that is, except Billy.

Billy raises his hand high. "Billy, do you have something to say?" asks Ms. Jenny.

"Is your dad wearing polka-dotted socks?" he asks.

I can feel my face turning bright red. I stand, trembling, waiting for the kids to laugh.

Billy kept on speaking, "And is your mom dressed up like a ghost?"

This is it. I am sure I'll be sent home.

"Ummmmmm, yes," I murmured.

Billy smiled. Slowly, he held up the picture of his family for the whole class to see. In the picture, his mom is dressed up as a green goblin

. . . And his dad is wearing purple polka dotted socks.

My family is special. Here are their names and why they are unique...